I'm Reading About The GRAND CANYON

GALLOPADE

by Carole Marsh

Printed and Manufactured in Peachtree City, GA., USA www.gallopade.com

Book design: Susan Van Denhende

Editor: Janice Baker

The Grand Canyon
is a great place to visit!

What is so special about
the Grand Canyon?

Let's read about it and see!

INTRODUCTION

What is the Grand Canyon?

The Grand Canyon is a deep canyon
made of many layers of rock.
The Colorado River runs through the bottom.
The Colorado River carved the Grand Canyon!

The Grand Canyon

LOCATION

The Grand Canyon is located in Arizona.

Fast Facts About Arizona:

- Sixth largest state
- Capital is Phoenix
- 48th state to join the United States
- Nickname is "The Grand Canyon State"

Located in Arizona

NATIONAL PARK

The Grand Canyon is protected in Grand Canyon National Park.

What is a national park?

A national park is a large area of land set aside by a country. The land is kept natural and pure. Animals roam free.

National parks are fun for people to visit and enjoy!

Park Entrance

HISTORY

The Grand Canyon is home to
many Native American groups.
Native Americans have lived in and around the canyon
for thousands of years!

Native Americans include:

Havasupai **Navajo** **Hualapai** **Hopi** **Paiute**

Havasupai means "people of the blue-green waters."

Native Americans

Havasupai woman making baskets, circa 1900

HISTORY

In 1869, a group of men explored the Grand Canyon. Major John Wesley Powell was their leader.

They traveled in boats down the Colorado River. Major Powell gave the canyon its name!

Major Powell had only one arm. He lost his right arm during the Civil War.

Exploring the Canyon

SIZE

The Grand Canyon is HUGE!
You have got to see it to believe it!

Grand Canyon Fast Facts:

- 277 miles long
- Up to 18 miles wide
- More than one mile deep

The Grand Canyon has a North Rim and a South Rim. Most people visit the South Rim.

Colossal Canyon

WEATHER

The Grand Canyon has warm weather in the summer and cold weather in the winter.

At the bottom of the canyon, summer temperatures can get really hot—often higher than 100 degrees!

The canyon is cold.
The canyon is hot.
But whenever you go,
you'll like it a lot!

Weather

Colorado River

I am the Colorado River!
I flow at the bottom of the Grand Canyon.

Early Native Americans living in the canyon depended on me to survive.
Today, visitors enjoy boating and floating on my blue-green waters!

The Colorado River flows west through the canyon.

RIVER

Havasu Falls

I am Havasu Falls.
I am the most famous waterfall in the Grand Canyon!

Sunlight + minerals in the water
+ limestone in the riverbed
give my water its turquoise color!

Havasu Falls is in Havasu Canyon.
It is a side branch of the Grand Canyon.
The Havasupai people live here.

WATERFALL

Bighorn Sheep

I am a bighorn sheep!
I live in the Grand Canyon.
You may see me on cliffs and steep terrain.
I like to climb and I am very good at it!

You can tell I am a male
because I have big curved horns.
I am known as a "ram."

My female friends have short horns.
They are known as "ewes."

Mountain Lion

I am a mountain lion!
I am the largest predator in the Grand Canyon.

I only eat meat.
Some of the animals I eat
are elk, deer, and even bighorn sheep!
I am very sneaky and usually hunt at night.

Do you want to hear me roar?
I do not roar, but I can hiss, spit, growl, and purr.
Grrrrrrrrrrr...

Animals

elk

ringtail

falcon

scorpion

coyote

gila monster

There are many more animals
in the Grand Canyon!

There are tall ones like elk and mule deer.
There are small ones like ringtails and skunks.
There are flying ones like falcons and bats.
There are creeping ones like scorpions and tarantulas!

Outdoor Fun

THINGS TO DO

There many things to do
at the Grand Canyon!

Hike **Ride Mules** **Raft** **Camp** **Take Pictures** **Fish**

Whatever you choose,
you will have fun!
The canyon has activities
for everyone!

Scenic Rides

I am a helicopter!
I fly visitors over the Grand Canyon every day.
I think it is the best way to see the canyon.
What a fantastic view!

Small airplanes also take visitors on Grand Canyon tours. Look out, birds!

Grand Canyon Skywalk

I am the Grand Canyon Skywalk!
You will find me on the far western end
of the Grand Canyon.

I am a bridge shaped like a horseshoe.
I extend 70 feet out over the Grand Canyon.
My floor is made of glass.
You can see the canyon FAR below!

The Skywalk is on the Hualapai Indian Reservation.

Grand Canyon

DID YOU KNOW?

Read these fascinating facts about the Grand Canyon!

- It is one of the Seven Natural Wonders of the World.
- About five million people visit every year.
- Minerals in the rocks cause the striped colors.
- It took millions of years for the canyon to form.
- It has some of the cleanest air in the United States.

GLOSSARY

limestone: a rock formed mainly from animal remains like shells or coral

mineral: a substance (such as coal or quartz) that is naturally formed under the ground

predator: an animal that lives by killing and eating other animals

ringtail: a raccoon–like mammal with a bushy tail marked with black and white rings

survive: to remain alive

tarantula: a large, hairy spider

terrain: the specific physical features of an area of land

turquoise: a greenish–blue color